The Story of Nilima Gaul Bej

Rahul Maity

Ukiyoto Publishing

All global publishing rights are held by
Ukiyoto Publishing
Published in 2024

Content Copyright © Rahul Maity
ISBN 9789364949347
All rights reserved.
No part of this publication may be reproduced, transmitted, or stored in a retrieval system, in any form by any means, electronic, mechanical, photocopying, recording or otherwise, without the prior permission of the publisher.

The moral rights of the author have been asserted.

This book is sold subject to the condition that it shall not by way of trade or otherwise, be lent, resold, hired out or otherwise circulated, without the publisher's prior consent, in any form of binding or cover other than that in which it is published.

www.ukiyoto.com

Dedication

Nilima Bej

(2nd November 1951-3rd February 2024)

This book is dedicated to my Late grandmother Nilima Bej.

Preface

This book is about late Nilima Gaul Bej a gymnast of West Bengal who was extremely talented in gymnastics, the book revolves around the story of her talent, her achievements and how she entered the world of gymnastics.

Contents

Chapter 1 : About Nilima	1
Chapter 2 : History of Chapatala Youngmens Gymnastic Club	4
Chapter 3 : Excellency in Gymnastics	7
Chapter 4 : Golden Opportunities	10
Chapter 5 : Awards and Recognitions	13
Chapter 6 : Friends for Lifetime	26
Chapter 7: Love is in the Air	27
Chapter 8: Life After Gymnastics	28
Chapter 9: Photo Gallery of Nilima Gaul Bej	33
About the Author	*40*

Chapter 1 : About Nilima

Nilima, a bright star of the Bengal's gymnastic world, gifted with excellent talent was born on 2nd of November 1951 at Rajani Gupto Row of Central Kolkata to Naren Gaul and Nihar Gaul. She grew up with four siblings - her elder brother Riben Gaul, her elder sister Anjali Gaul Dhar, her younger sister Ashima Gaul Kundu and her younger brother Biren Gaul.

Childhood Picture of Nilima Gaul Bej

Nilima's father Naren Gaul had an immense contribution to Nilima's gymnastic career. Naren Gaul was himself a gymnastic coach. Nilima was born into a wealthy and happy family, her childhood days were spent with extreme joy, laughter and by creating sweet and lovely memories.

Nilima Gaul got her education from Loreto Convent Entally and from Madhya Kalikata Balika Vidyalaya. But rather than studies she got more interested in the sports field mainly in gymnastics, and this interest in gymnastics was developed by her father, coach Naren gaul.

Not only Nilima but also her sister Ashima Gaul got interested in gymnastics, so they both started to follow the path shown by their father. The two sisters got so much interest in gymnastics they started practicing gymnastics regularly. Both of the sisters not only used to practice gymnastics together but also they shared a very good sibling bond with each other.

Nilima Gaul with her parents and siblings

Chapter 2 : History of Chapatala Youngmens Gymnastic Club

In Central Kolkata, there is an area known as Chapatala, now in this Chapatala area there is a lane named Akhil Mistri Lane. But why should we know about all this ??, because this is the place where India's first gymnastic club was established and it was named as Chapatala Youngmens Gymnastic Club. The club was established by Chunilal Pramanik.

This is the place where Nilima got training in gymnastics under the guidance of her father Coach Naren Gaul. Coach Naren Gaul was the one who made Chapatala Youngmens Gymnastic Club popular on those days. But nowadays if you go to find this club you would not be able to find it because now the club has become extinct. This was one of the oldest gymnastic clubs but now there is no sign of its existence.

Coach Naren Gaul - Father of Nilima Gaul Bej

At that time the club was this much popular that various countries like Japan, Russia, berlin knew about this gymnastic club. Most popular women gymnasts of this club were Nilma Gaul, Ashima Gaul and Ambalika Mazumdar. Huge crowd of people used to come to watch their different types of gymnastic stunts at a place name Sraddhananda park where they used to perform gymnastics.

At that time the two girls Nilima Gaul and Ashima Gaul were known as 'Plastic Girls', there is a reason behind the name given to them, when they used to perform gymnastic, they performed it in such a way it looked like that there is any bone present in their body, they were only made of muscles.

Chapter 3 : Excellency in Gymnastics

Coach Naren Gaul always had a belief that without giving training to her own daughters he will be unable to attract interest of other girls in the field of gymnastics. That's why Nilima and Ashima started practicing gymnastics under the guidance of their father. And in this way Nilima Gaul entered the world of gymnastics.

Nilima Gaul Bej doing gymnastic stunts

Nilima Gaul not only entered the gymnastic world but also gained immense popularity through her excellent talent in gymnastics.

Nilima Gaul participated and showed excellency in various gymnastic championship - XII National Championship, 1966, winter games organised by School Games Federation of India, 11th National Gymnastic Championship of India, 1967, Rupar, organised by Gymnastic Federation of India, XII National Gymnastic Championship, 1967, Agartala Tripura, organised by Gymnastic Federation of India, Gymnastic Competition organised by West Bengal Lenin Centenary Youth Festival Preparatory Committee, 1970, XIIIth National Gymnastic Championship of India, 1970, Cuttack.

Chapter 4 : Golden Opportunities

After all of those achievements comes one golden opportunity in her life, a letter from Honorary Secretary Broja Ranjan Roy of Gymnastic Federation of India which stated that Nilima Gaul was selected by the executive committee of the Gymnastic Federation of India for training at National Institute of Sports, Patiala through which she can get selected for the final selected team to participate in Mexico Games.

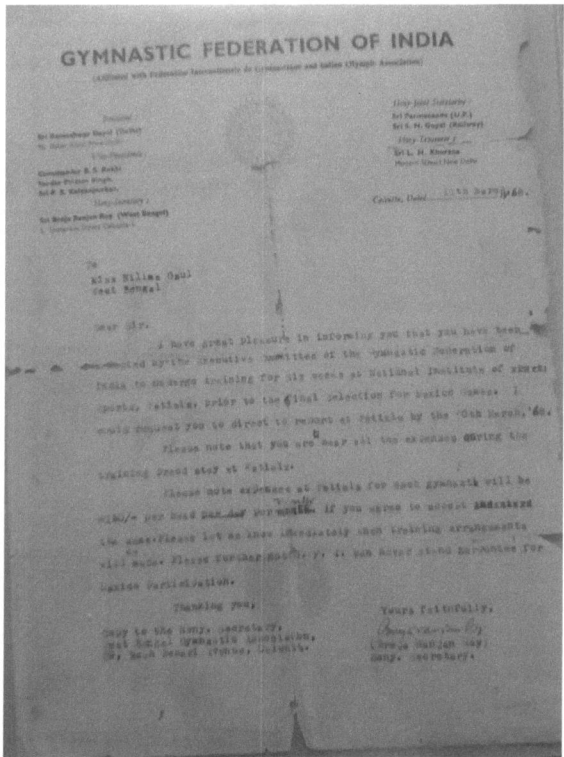

Letter for the Training from Gymnastic Federation of India

After this in 1971 she was selected to undergo training for First Asian Youth Gymnastics Championship in Tokyo Japan. And with many other gymnasts - Nilima also gets the training, but unfortunately during the training period she suffered from leg fracture and missed the opportunity of participating in First Asian Youth Gymnastics Championship.

Nilima Gaul with her sister Ashima Gaul and other gymnasts in the training camp for First Asian Youth Gymnastics Championship

Chapter 5 : Awards and Recognitions

- Certificate received in Individual Championship in Women section representing West Bengal state in XII National Championship, 1966, Winter Games, Udaipur, 28th December 1966-1st January 1967, organised by Schools Games Federation of India.

Certificate received from Schools Games Federation of India in XII National Championship,1966, Winter Games

- Certificate received in events Floor Exercises and Uneven Parallel Bar representing West Bengal state in Women section for securing 1st position in floor exercises with 9.35 points and for securing second position in Uneven Parallel Bar with 8.10 points in 11th National Gymnastic Championship of India, 1967, Rupar, 6th-8th February, 1967, organised by Gymnastic Federation of India.

14   The Story of Nilima Gaul Bej

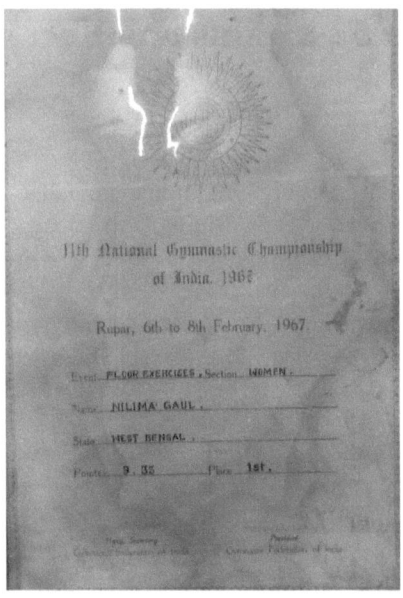

Certificate Received from Gymnastic Federation of India in 11th National Gymnastic Championship of India, 1967

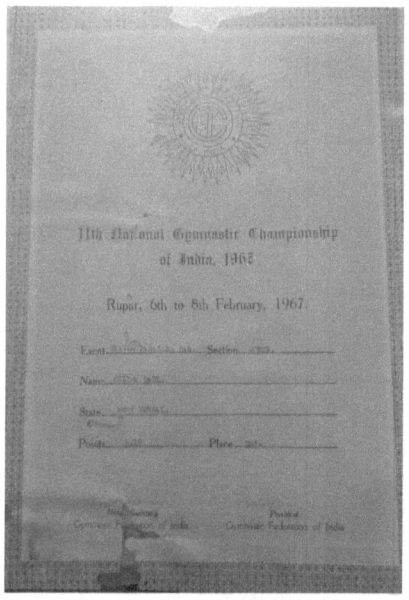

Certificate Received from Gymnastic Federation of India in 11th National Gymnastic Championship of India, 1967

- Certificate received in events Beam Balancing, Floor Exercise and All Round Individual Champion representing West Bengal state in Women Section for securing 1st position in Floor Exercise with 9.45 points, for securing 1st position in Beam Balancing with 9.25 points and for securing 1st position in All Round Individual Champion in XII National Championship, 1967, Agartala Tripura, 17th-23rd December, 1967 organised by Gymnastic Federation of India.

The Story of Nilima Gaul Bej

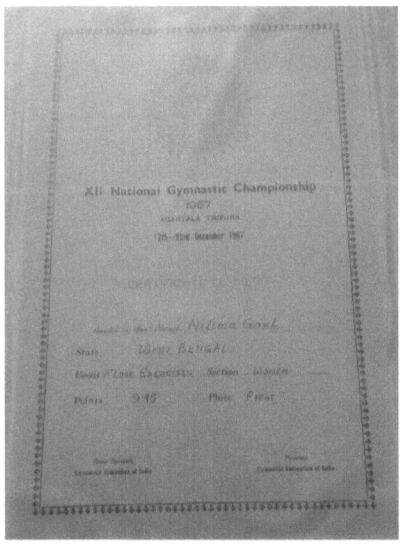

Certificate received from Gymnastic Federation of India in XII National Championship, 1967

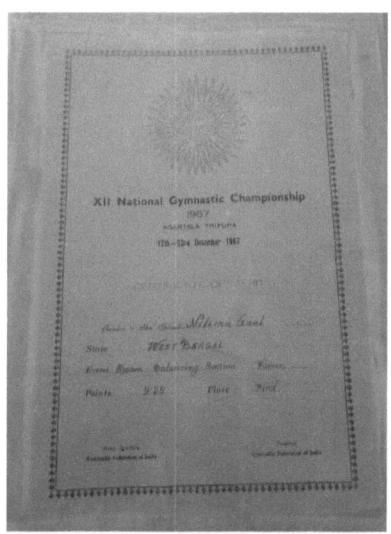

Certificate received from Gymnastic Federation of India in XII National Championship, 1967

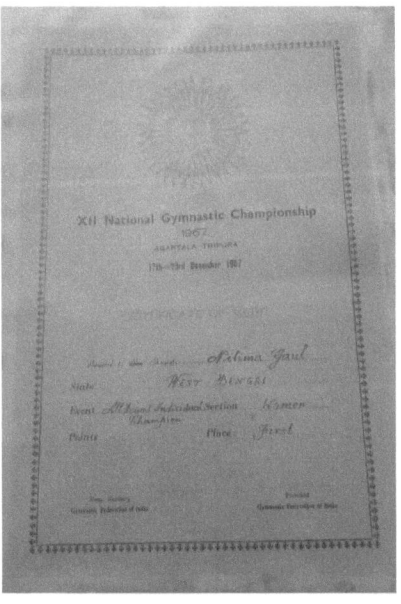

Certificate received from Gymnastic Federation of India in XII National Championship, 1967

- Certificate received in events Beam Balance and Floor Exercise representing West Bengal state in Women section for securing 2nd position in Floor Exercise with 8.20 points and for securing 2nd position in Beam Balance with 8.30 points in XIIIth National Gymnastic Championship, 1970, Cuttack, 14th-18th January, 1970, organised by Gymnastic Federation of India.

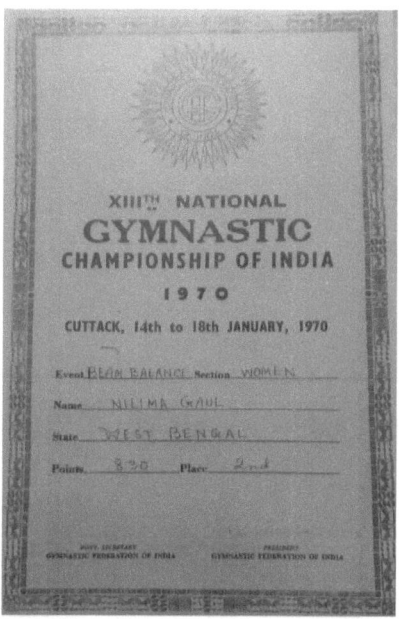

Certificate received from Gymnastic Federation of India in XIIIth National Championship, 1967

20 The Story of Nilima Gaul Bej

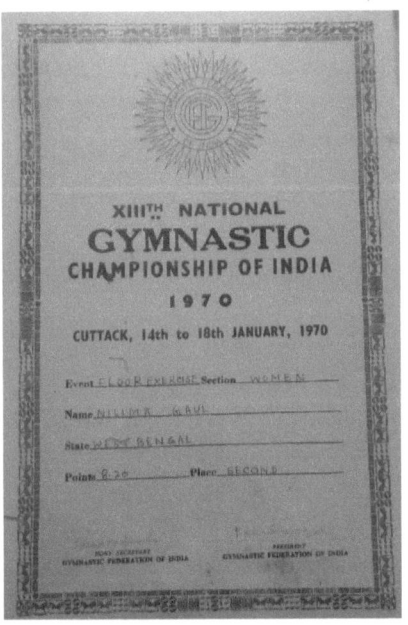

Certificate received from Gymnastic Federation of India in XIIIth National Championship, 1967

- Certificate received in events Beam Balance, Voalting Horse and Floor Exercise in Women section for securing 1st position in Beam Balance, for securing 1st position in Voalting Horse and for securing 1st position in Floor Exercise in Gymnastic Competition, 1970 organised by West Bengal Lenin Centenary Youth Preparatory Committee.

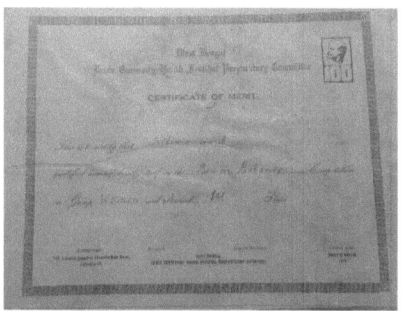

Certificate received from West Bengal Lenin
Centenary Youth Preparatory Committee

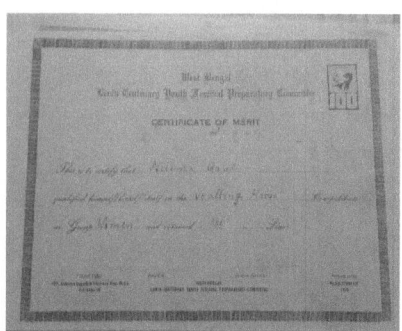

Certificate received from West Bengal Lenin
Centenary Youth Preparatory Committee

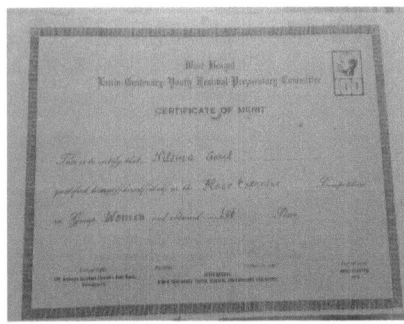

Certificate received from West Bengal Lenin Centenary Youth Preparatory Committee

- Certificate received for passing the test held in December 1989, in acquiring the skill Machine Embroidery from Brahmo Samaj Mahila Bhaban Shilpa Vidyalaya.

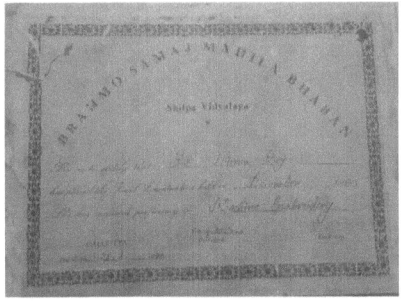

Certificate received in Machine Embroidery from Brahmo Samaj Mahila Bhaban Shilpa Vidyalaya

- Received award from West Bengal Gymnastic Association for glorious deeds in gymnastics

Award received from West Bengal Gymnastic Association

- Felicitation received for great achievements in Gymnastics

24 The Story of Nilima Gaul Bej

Felicitation received for achievement in gymnastics

Medals awarded to Nilima Gaul Bej

Chapter 6 : Friends for Lifetime

By nature, Nilima was very friendly with which she made a number of good friends which became her friends for lifetime. When Nilima was studying at Loreto Convent, she made two friends Shikha and Minoti and they were friends from her nursery class. At the time of departure from the school Nilima and Minoti used to go to Shikha's Home. there were Falsa (Indian Summer Berries) trees in the garden of Shikha's House, three of them used to climb those trees and pluck out those fruits to eat them. Shikha's mother used to prepare "Kuler Achar" for them and they all used to have them with lots of joy.

During Nilima's Gymnastic career she made two more good friends Arati Das and Ambalika Majumdar, not only two, but she also made three good friends, another one was Ashit Kumar Bej. Nilima used to save money from the money from her tiffin and used to buy tiffin for her friend Ambalika. Nilima used to buy "Danadar" sweet and "Bheli Gur" for her friend Ambalika. Ashit Kumar Bej later became Nilima's Brother-in-law.

Chapter 7: Love is in the Air

Chunilal Bej, the eldest son of the Bej family fell in love at first sight with Nilima Gaul. To watch Nilima Chunilal started visiting the gymnastic club daily with his younger brother Ashit Kumar Bej, who was Nilima's friend also. Now Chunilal also got admission in that gymnastic club, but he didn't do any gymnastic, he just did freehand exercises, Chunilal's actual motive was to get a sight of Nilima on daily basis and he will be satisfied with that, such a romantic gesture isn't it!!!

But now the question is how they did both fell in love with each other, one day Chunilal was riding a bike showing his biking skills to everyone at the locality of Nilima, during which he met with a minor accident and got a leg injury. Now, Nilima took him to her home and started treating her leg injury with great care through which they both deeply fell in love with each other.

After falling in love with each other, both decided to get married to each other. so, both of them told their families about this, Chunilal's family got convinced but Nilima's family was not convinced easily. Nilima's elder sister Anjali Dhar helped Nilima to convince her family, and with the help of her elder sister Nilima succeeded in convincing her family for the marriage.

Chapter 8: Life After Gymnastics

Nilima Gaul continued her gymnastic career till 1973, after that she got married to Chunilal Bej on 3rd March 1973 and gained a new title 'Boro Bou' of Bej Bari and became Nilima Bej from Nilima Gaul. Chunilal and Nilima had a love marriage, she got married into a wealthy family, the Bej family was a joint family and till date they are still a joint family. After marriage her new residence became Prem Chand Baral lane of Central Kolkata.

Nilima Bej with her husband Chunilal Bej

In 1974 she became mother of a daughter named Merry and in 1975 of a son named Sanjib. As Nilima herself was in the sports field she wanted her son and daughter also to be in the sports field. So, she made her daughter get training in swimming and made her son get training in Rifle Shooting. She put an immense effort in order to make her son a Rifle Shooter and to make her daughter a swimmer and she got success and made her daughter a swimmer and her son a Rifle Shooter.

Nilima Bej with her Husband Chunilal Bej, Daughter Merry Maity, son Sanjib Bej

Nilima loved her daughter and Son and cared about them a lot. In this respect it should be mentioned that she loved her son in law Manoranjan Maity like her own son, she treated and cared about him like her own son. Manoranjan and Nilima shared a great bonding with each other like mother and son. Nilima had a great bonding with her granddaughter Sohini Maity and her grandson Rahul Maity.

She was a great cook, and really loved to cook for her family. She developed an interest in sewing and stitching and got training from Brahmo Samaj Mahila Bhaban Shilpa Vidyalaya and she also developed interest in learning driving and started learning driving. She always had an interest in learning new things. Nilima Bej was a great devotee of Maa Kali; his husband is also a great devotee of Maa Kali. Nilima Bej and Chunilal Bej both founded a Kali temple named Sealdah Kalibari at Fordyce Lane on 22nd January 2004, where every year a grand celebration is celebrated annually.

Sealdah Kalibari founded by Chunilal Bej & Nilima Bej

In April 2023 she suffered a mild brain stroke but her fighter spirit completely recovered from that and became completely fit. But who knew that she is only left with a few months of her life, in October, 2023 she again fell sick and got admitted in hospital and this time doctor detected urine infection which had turned into sepsis and later caused septic shock leading to multiorgan failure.

After October 2023, day by day she kept falling more and more sick until she reached her deathbed. Lots and lots of treatment was done to her but still her health deteriorated day by day. Her fighter spirit lost her last breath ending the battle of 4 months and left for her heavenly abode on 3rd February, 2024. Her last rites were performed by her family at Nimtala Shamshan Ghat, Kolkata on 4th February, 2024.

Chapter 9: Photo Gallery of Nilima Gaul Bej

The Story of Nilima Gaul Bej

Rahul Maity

36   The Story of Nilima Gaul Bej

38 The Story of Nilima Gaul Bej

Rahul Maity

About the Author

Rahul Maity

Rahul Maity is a Graduate in B.com Honors in Accounting & Finance, completed his graduation from Prafulla Chandra College, Kolkata. He completed his schooling from Nava Nalanda High School, Kolkata.

www.ingramcontent.com/pod-product-compliance
Lightning Source LLC
LaVergne TN
LVHW041558070526
838199LV00046B/2030